To ....

From ....

Date ....

WITH YOU ALL THE WAY

Illustrations by
CHUCK GILLIES

MAX
LUCADO

CROSSWAY BOOKS · WHEATON, ILLINOIS

A DIVISION OF GOOD NEWS PUBLISHERS

Publisher's Acknowledgments

The publisher wishes to acknowledge that the text for *With You All the Way*
appeared originally as "Song of the King" in *Tell Me the Secrets,* written by Max Lucado and
illustrated by Ron DiCianni. Special thanks to Ron DiCianni for the idea and vision behind the
creation of the "Tell Me" series. Look for more stories in the series— *Tell Me the Story, Tell Me the
Secrets, Tell Me the Truth, Tell Me the Promises,* and *Tell Me Why,*
all published by Crossway Books—at your local bookstore.

WITH YOU ALL THE WAY

Text copyright © 1993, 1995, 2000 by Max Lucado

Illustrations copyright © 2000 by Chuck Gillies

Published by Crossway Books

a division of Good News Publishers

1300 Crescent Street

Wheaton, Illinois 60187

Cover illustration: Chuck Gillies

Design: Uttley/DouPonce DesignWorks, www.uddesignworks.com

Edited by Karen Hill

First printing 1995, new edition 2000

Printed in the United States of America

LIBRARY OF CONGRESS CATALOGING-IN-PUBLICATION DATA

Lucado, Max.

[Song of the King]
With You All the Way / Max Lucado: illustrated by Chuck Gillies.
p. cm.
Summary: Three knights set out on a perilous journey to reach the king's castle, but the only
one to reach his goal is the one who was wise enough to listen to the song of the king.
[1. Knights and knighthood--Fiction. 2. Kings, queens, rulers, etc.—Fiction. 3. Parables.] I. Gillies,
Chuck, 1950- ill. II. Title.
PZ7.L9684Wi 2000   [Fic]—dc21   00-057051

ISBN 1-58134-210-1

08	07	06	05	04	03	02	01	00
15	14	13	12	11	10	9	8	7	6	5	4	3	2	1

Dedicated with love to J.T., Carrigan, and Tyler

May you hear the song of the King.

Three knights sat at a table and listened as their prince spoke.

"My father, the king, will give the hand of my sister to the first of you who can prove himself worthy."

The prince paused to let the men take in the news. He looked at their faces—each weathered from miles and scarred from battles. The three had much in common. They were the strongest warriors in the kingdom, and they each wanted to marry the daughter of the king. The king had promised each a chance—a test to see which was worthy of his daughter. And now the time for the test had arrived.

"The test is a journey," the prince explained, "a journey to the king's castle by way of Hemlock."

"The forest?" one knight quickly inquired.

"The forest," answered the prince.

There was silence as the knights thought about the words. Each felt a stab of fear.

They knew the danger of Hemlock, a dark and deadly place. Parts of it were so thick with trees that the sunlight never found the ground.

It was home of the Hopenots—small, sly creatures with yellow eyes. Hopenots were not strong, but they were clever, and they were many. Some people believed the Hopenots were lost travelers changed by the darkness. But no one really knew for sure.

"Will we travel alone?" Carlisle spoke—a strange question to come from the strongest of the three knights. His fierce sword was known throughout the kingdom.

But even this steely soldier knew better than to travel Hemlock alone. "You may each choose one person to travel with you all the way to the castle."

"But the forest is dark. The trees make the sky black. How will we find the castle?" This time it was Alon who spoke. He was not as strong as Carlisle but much quicker.

He was famous for his speed. Alon left trails of confused enemies. He had escaped them by ducking into trees or scampering over walls. But quickness is worthless if you have no direction. So Alon asked, "How can we find the way?"

The prince nodded, reached into his sack, and pulled out an ivory flute. "There are only two of these," he explained. "This one and another in the possession of the king." He put the instrument to his lips and played a soft, sweet song. Never had the knights heard such soothing music.

"My father's flute plays the same song. His song will guide you to the castle."

"How is that?" Alon asked.

"Three times a day the king will play from the castle wall. Early in the morning, at noon, and again in the evening. Listen for him. Follow his song and you will find the castle."

"There is only one other flute like this one?"

"Only one."

"And you and your father play the same music?"

"Yes."

It was Cassidon who was asking. Cassidon was known for his alertness. He saw what others missed. He knew the home of a traveler by the dirt on his boot. He knew the truth of a story by the eyes of the teller. He could tell the size of a marching army by the number of scattered birds in flight.

Carlisle and Alon wondered why he asked about the flute. It wouldn't be very long before they found out.

"Consider the danger of Hemlock and wisely choose the one who will be with you on your journey," the prince cautioned.

And so they did. The next morning the three knights mounted their horses and entered Hemlock. Beside each rode the chosen companion.

For the people in the king's castle, the days of waiting passed slowly. All knew of the test. And all wondered which knight would win the princess. Three times a day the king sent his song soaring into the trees of Hemlock. And three times a day the people stopped their work to listen.

After many days and countless songs, a watchman spotted two figures stumbling out of the forest. No one could tell who they were. They were too far from the castle. The men had no horses, weapons, or armor.

"Hurry," the king commanded his guards, "bring them in. Give them medical treatment and food, but don't tell anyone who they are. Dress the knight as a prince, and we will see their faces tonight at the banquet."

He then dismissed the crowds and told them to prepare for the feast.

That evening a joyful spirit filled the banquet hall. At every table the people tried to guess which knight had survived Hemlock Forest.

Finally, the moment came to present the winner. At the king's signal the people became quiet, and he began to play the flute. Once again the ivory instrument sang. The people turned to see who would enter.

Many thought it would be Carlisle, the strongest. Others felt it would be Alon, the swiftest.

But it was neither. The knight who survived the journey was Cassidon, the wisest.

He strode quickly across the floor, following the sound of the flute one final time, and bowed before the king.

"Tell us of your journey," he was instructed. The people leaned forward to listen.

"The Hopenots were crafty," Cassidon began. "They attacked, but we fought back. They took our horses, but we continued. What nearly destroyed us, though, was something far worse."

"What was that?" asked the princess.

"They imitated."

"They imitated?" asked the king.

"Yes, my king. They imitated. Each time the song of your flute would enter the forest, a hundred flutes would begin to play. All around us we heard music—songs from every direction."

"I do not know what became of Carlisle and Alon," he continued, "but I know that strength and speed will not help one hear the right flute."

The king asked the question that was on everyone's lips. "Then how did you hear my song?"

"I chose the right companion," he answered as he motioned for his fellow traveler to enter. The people gasped.

It was the prince. In his hand he carried the flute.

"I knew there was only one who could play your song exactly like you," Cassidon explained. "There is no one else I would have trusted to be with me all the way. So I asked him to travel with me. As we journeyed, he played your song. I learned it so well that though a thousand false flutes tried to hide your music, I could hear your song above them all. It was with me all the way."

And with that, the celebration began.